Author's Note
This story is one of the many Law Tales of Burma. Each of these
Law Tales has a judgement by the Princess Learned-in-Law at
the end of it. The ridiculous tales that the animals tell have their
counterparts in nonsense stories told all around the world.

Copyright © Joanna Troughton 1991

First published in 1991 by
Blackie and Son Limited
7 Leicester Place
London WC2H 7BP

First American edition published in 1991 by
Peter Bedrick Books
2112 Broadway, New York, NY 10023

Library of Congress Cataloging-in-Publication Data
Troughton, Joanna.
    Make-believe tales : a folk tale from Burma / retold and
illustrated by Joanna Troughton -- 1st American ed.
        (Folk tales of the world)
    Summary: Four animals challenge a traveller to a tale-telling
contest, which Princess Learned-in-the-Law must adjudicate.
    ISBN 0-87226-451-3
    [1. Folklore -- Burma.]   I. Title.   II. Series: Folk tales of the
world (New York, N.Y.)
PZ8.1.T74Mak 1991
398.24′5′09591--dc   90-48962
[20]   CIP
                                                                   AC

Printed in Hong Kong by Wing King Tong Co. Ltd.

Make-Believe Tales

A Folk Tale from Burma

Retold and illustrated by
Joanna Troughton

Bedrick/Blackie
New York

There once lived a cat, a mouse, a parrot and a monkey. One day they met a rich traveller. 'Let us make a bet with him,' said the cat. 'We shall bet him all his fine clothes and the riches he carries that he won't believe the tales we will tell him.' The traveller agreed to this bet and the cat began his tale. . .

'One day I went fishing and I couldn't catch any fish.

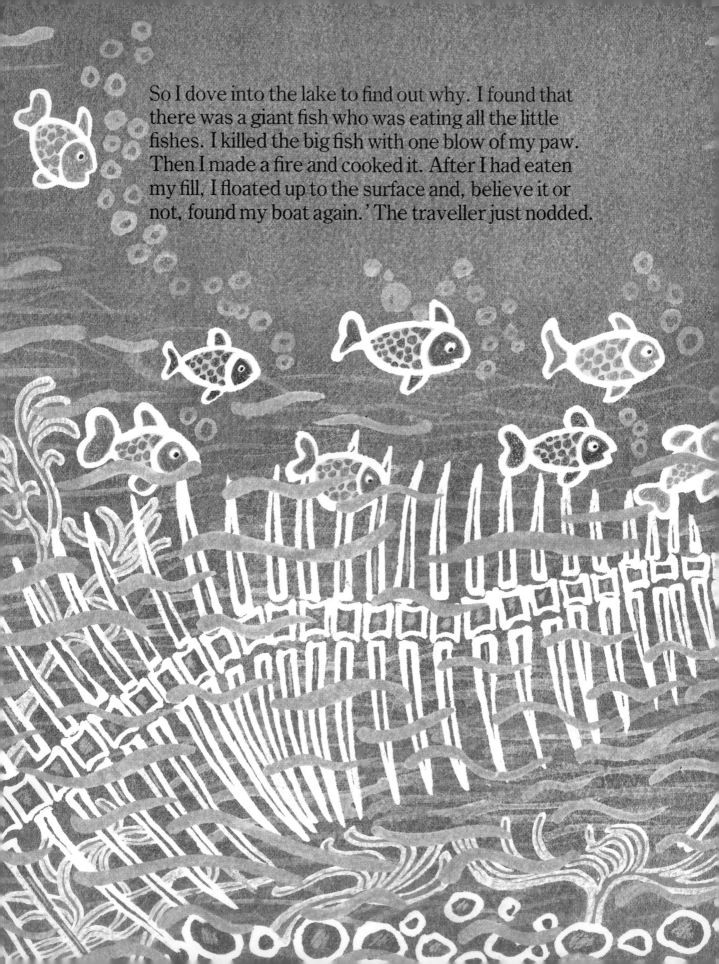

So I dove into the lake to find out why. I found that there was a giant fish who was eating all the little fishes. I killed the big fish with one blow of my paw. Then I made a fire and cooked it. After I had eaten my fill, I floated up to the surface and, believe it or not, found my boat again.' The traveller just nodded.

The mouse then told his tale. 'One day I was out in the jungle when suddenly I came face to face with a huge tiger.

He opened his mouth and gobbled me up.
But I was so strong that I forced the
tiger's mouth open and, believe it or not,
jumped out unharmed.' The traveller
just nodded.

Next the parrot told his tale. 'One day a girl asked me to pick some mangoes that grew high up in a tree. I flew up and took the mangoes back to her in my beak.

The girl ate her fill, but there were so many mangoes left over that she piled the rest outside her house and, believe it or not, the pile was so high that it reached her window.' The traveller just nodded.

Then the monkey told his tale. 'One day while swinging from a tree I missed my footing and nearly fell. Luckily an elephant with his driver passed below me, so I asked them for help.

The elephant driver reached up
to rescue me, but as he did so the
elephant walked away. . .

. . . leaving us both dangling from the tree.

I asked the elephant driver to sing a song to attract attention. And, believe it or not, the song was so good that I had to clap.

So we both fell to earth with a bump.'
The traveller just nodded.

'Now I will tell you a tale,' the traveller said. The animals were dismayed. They hadn't thought it was a two-way bet. But the traveller began his tale. 'One day on my farm there grew a large cotton plant. After a while it bore four pods. When the pods were ripe they burst. . .

. . . and out jumped a cat, a mouse, a parrot and a monkey. As the cotton plant belonged to me, the animals were my slaves and went to work on my farm. But one day they ran away and, believe it or not, I have been looking for them ever since. At last I have found you!' said the traveller.

The cat, the mouse, the parrot and the monkey
were silent. If they said they didn't believe the
traveller's tale then they had lost their bet. If they
said they believed his story then they were his slaves.

The cat, the mouse, the parrot, the monkey and the traveller went to the Princess-Learned-in-Law for a judgement. The Princess-Learned-in-Law listened to their case and then she said, 'You cannot change a bet at the end of a game. The bet was for the fine clothes the traveller wore and the riches he carried. He has won the bet, so let him take only the fine clothes that the animals wear and the riches they carry. That is my judgement in the case of the Make-Believe Tales.'